DAVID LYON

The Runaway

Duck

Lothrop, Lee & Shepard Books   New York

Printed in the United States of America.

First Edition
4   5   6   7   8   9   10   11   12   13   14   15

Library of Congress Cataloging-in-Publication Data

Lyon, David.
     The runaway duck.

     Summary: Sebastian's pull-toy duck, Egbert, has many
adventures after Sebastian ties him to the bumper of his
father's car.
     [1. Toys—Fiction]   I. Title.
PZ7.L99528Ru 1985   [E]   84-5677
ISBN 0-688-04002-0
ISBN 0-688-04003-9 (lib. bdg.)

To Mel and Rosemary

One morning, Sebastian Willowfrost was playing in the garage. He was rolling Egbert, his favorite toy, around on the floor.

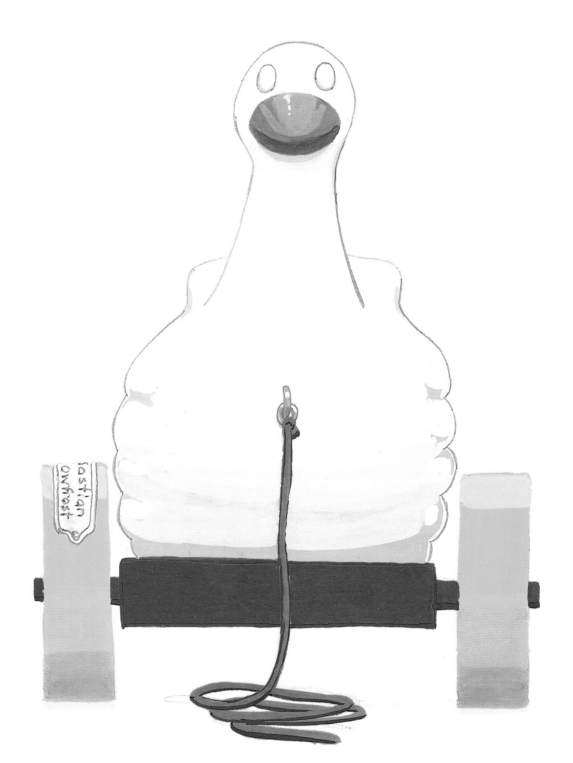

Egbert was a carved wooden duck with wheels and
a long nylon string for pulling. The wheels were mounted
on metal axles and rolled very smoothly. One wheel had a
plaque on which Sebastian had written his name.

Suddenly, Sebastian's father, Albert Willowfrost, called him in for lunch.

"Just a minute," cried Sebastian.

Sebastian tied Egbert to the bumper of his father's car so that he couldn't roll away.

Lunch was sandwiches and soup.

Sebastian's father ate quickly, wiped his face with a napkin, kissed Sebastian's mother good-bye, and hugged Sebastian. He was going on a long business trip and wouldn't be back for a week.

Sebastian forgot that Egbert was tied to the bumper of his father's car.

By the time Sebastian remembered, Egbert was doing sixty miles an hour down Route 95. The road was rough, and Egbert bounced all over.

Racing around a sharp mountain turn,
Egbert's tie string broke.
Egbert sailed off, underneath the guard rail
and into empty space.

For ten seconds, Egbert flew like a real duck.
But then he fell—down, down, down—into
Emerald Valley.

Luckily, Egbert fell into a stream, where he was carried forward by the force of the water.

The fish in the stream thought this was funny—such a strange duck with wooden wheels!

Egbert rolled and floated on,
past Steelburg,
Bottleburg,
Carburg,
and Burgerburg—
out into Burtlebaum Bay and the sea.

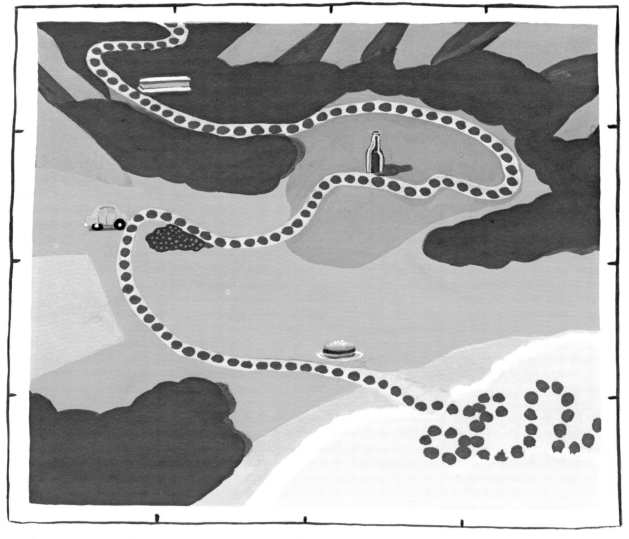

●●●●● PATH OF THE DUCK

An eagle-eyed sailor on board
the *S.S. Rover* spotted Egbert
and tried to rescue him, but a
sudden typhoon drove the ship away.

Meanwhile, Sebastian prayed that Egbert was safe and that he might return. He wrote several poems in memory of Egbert and tried to forget the whole tragedy by playing baseball with the Indian family from across the street.

One night in early September, Egbert was attacked by a shark.

The shark pulled Egbert down into the ocean. He bit off one of Egbert's wheels, discovered that it was wood, and swam away in disgust.

Egbert floated up—past a clown fish, a sea turtle, and a puff fish. The wheel floated up alone.

After some time, a wave tossed Egbert onto an almost deserted isle.

"Voila, un canard!"* cried Jacques Divan, poet, shipwreck survivor and Frenchman.

*This is French for "Whoopee! A duck!"

Jacques wrote a long poem about Egbert,
called "Song to a Duck." The poem begins:

Oh, what luck,
to find a duck,
upon a desert isle.

He's missing a wheel,
and his paint's all peeled,
but nevertheless
he smiles!

Time passed slowly. Sebastian and Jacques continued to pray and write poems.

One night, a shooting star brightened Jacques' island, and Sebastian awoke from the middle of a dream.

The next day, sailors on a French merchant vessel
spotted Jacques and carried him and Egbert to France.

There was much excitement over the castaways.
The president of France met the ship at port.

Le Monde, an important French newspaper, published
a photo of Egbert and a copy of Jacques' poem.

Sebastian happened to see Egbert's picture at a local newsstand while buying some gum.

He immediately went home and wrote a letter to the president of France, enclosing an old photo of Egbert and a couple of his poems.

"Please," he wrote, "send Egbert home."

Jacques was enjoying dinner when the French president showed him the letter, the photo, and the poems. Jacques tossed his napkin on the table and stood up.

"But this is my duck," Jacques cried. "Why, they are not the same; they cannot be!"

The president's daughter urged him to return the duck.

Jacques went for a long walk around the Eiffel Tower.
He realized Sebastian's poems were better than his own,
and that the wooden duck was probably Sebastian's after all.

Meanwhile, the president's daughter checked to see
whether Sebastian's name was on Egbert's right front wheel,
as Sebastian claimed in his letter. Unfortunately, this wheel was
now in Portugal, where a little girl was wearing it on a necklace.

When he got back to the palace, Jacques announced,
"I will return the duck this evening by air post."

The president's daughter kissed Jacques on the cheek.

Sebastian received the package and a letter two weeks
later.

Jacques and the French president's daughter were going
to be married. They invited Sebastian and his family to
the wedding.

Everything seemed perfect. Jacques had been rescued.
Egbert had returned. And the Willowfrost family would see
a French wedding.

Sometimes, though, Sebastian tried to imagine what had
happened to Egbert's front wheel.

And sometimes, far, far away, a little girl in Portugal
wondered just who Sebastian Willowfrost was.